Around the Passover Table

illustrated by

Tracy Newman **Adriana Santos**

Albert Whitman & Company
Chicago, Illinois

To Mom, for always
believing in me—TN

To my beloved family,
thanks for constant support
and enthusiasm—AS

Library of Congress Cataloging-in-Publication data is on file with the publisher.

Text copyright © 2019 by Tracy Newman
Pictures copyright © 2019 by Albert Whitman & Company
Pictures by Adriana Santos
First published in the United States of America in 2019 by Albert Whitman & Company
ISBN 978-0-8075-0446-8
Printed in China
10 9 8 7 6 5 4 3 2 1 NP 22 21 20 19 18

Design by Ellen Kokontis

For more information about Albert Whitman & Company,
visit our website at www.albertwhitman.com.

100 Years of Albert Whitman & Company
Celebrate with us in 2019!

Here is our table for this seder night.

With fresh springtime flowers and once-a-year dishes,
Two candles stand straight
See our grand seder plate

At our table for this seder night.

We add comfy pillows to chairs where we sit
Like royals reclining
Leaning while dining

At our table for this seder night.

There—in the center, lies grape juice so yummy

First one cup, then more

We drink two, three, then four

At our table for this seder night.

Next to the grape juice, we've put out the water

Hands—one, two—we wash

Pour some, *splish, splosh*

At our table for this seder night.

Alongside that pitcher, our salt water stands
Dip *karpas*, *swish*, *swish*
Take turns, pass the dish

At our table for this seder night.

And next to our *karpas*, three *matzos* are stacked
The middle one's split
We'll go searching for it

At our table for this seder night.

Close by those *matzos*, our *Haggadah* rests
Its tale we recite
Asking, "Why on this night?"

At our table for this seder night.

And after Four Questions,
with juice we count plagues
One drop, then again
Until we have ten

At our table for this seder night.

And next, sing *Dayenu*, our bright, festive song
Rejoice—voices loud
Give thanks—we're so proud

At our table for this seder night.

Pour out some water, we wash hands again—
Then our first *matzo* bite
So crunchy and light

At our table for this seder night.

Next take *charoset* and the *maror*
Dip bitter in sweet
Hold them and eat

At our table for this seder night.

Almost last but not least, we're ready. Let's feast!
Singing and sipping,
Laughing and dipping

At our table for this seder night.

Let's search for the *afikomen*. Ready, set, go!
Kids scramble and scatter
"The cushions!" "That platter!"

At our table for this seder night.

And now welcome guests to drink from their cups
We swing the door wide
Ask Elijah inside
Fill Miriam's cup
Lift it high. Lift it up.

As friends and family delight
At our table, our joyous, most glorious table...
For this sacred seder night.

Author's Note

Passover, called *Pesach* in Hebrew, is an eight-day festival that takes place every spring. This holiday celebrates the Jewish people's liberation from slavery in Egypt thousands of years ago. On the first two nights of Passover (and in some families, also the last two nights), people come together to read, sing, eat, pray, and celebrate at a gathering called a seder.

The seder begins at sundown and sets out a specific series and structure of steps to be followed. In fact, the word seder means "order" in Hebrew.

But seders are also festive, lively occasions in which children are told stories, encouraged to ask questions, eat special food, and even embark on a treasure hunt. Growing up, Passover seders were one of my favorite Jewish celebrations. I loved feasting on Passover-only treats like *charoset*, crowding around an extra-long table with my cousins, giggling and reading the *Haggadah*, competing to find the *afikomen* (which my grandfather always hid under the tablecloth), and ending the evening with a belly full of jelly candies and chocolate lollipops.

I hope that reading about the Passover table and exploring the distinctive elements that are featured in the seder helps you and your family experience and savor the excitement and joy that this festive holiday brings every year.

Here are some key terms used during the Passover seder:

afikomen (or afikoman)—the half-piece of matzo that is hidden and then eaten at the end of the seder

charoset—a mixture of chopped apples, nuts, and grape juice that represents the bricks used by Jewish people when they were slaves in Egypt

Dayenu—a spirited song sung during the seder meaning "it would have been enough" that expresses the Jewish people's gratitude for the gifts they have received throughout history

The Four Questions—a series of questions sung by the youngest child at the seder asking why this night is different from all other nights

Haggadah—the book that provides a guide to the seder, containing the Passover story, prayers, blessings, and songs

karpas—a vegetable, such as parsley, that symbolizes springtime and is dipped in salt water at the seder to represent the Jewish people's hard labor as slaves in Egypt

maror—bitter herbs such as romaine lettuce, celery, or horseradish that are eaten at the seder to symbolize the bitterness the Jewish people felt as slaves

matzo (or matzoh, matzah)—unleavened bread that is eaten during the eight days of Passover to symbolize the Jewish people rushing to leave Egypt so quickly that they couldn't wait for their bread to rise